Big Boys Sleep in Their Beds

NETA FAYNBOYM

Big Boys Sleep in Their Beds, Published August, 2015

Interior and Cover Illustrations: Randy Jennings
Interior Layout: Howard Johnson at Howard Communigrafix, Inc.
Editorial and Proofreading: Lisa Ann Schleipfer at Eden Rivers Editorial Services
and Karen Grennan
Photo Credit: Polina Faynboym

 SDP Publishing

Published by SDP Publishing, an imprint of SDP Publishing Solutions, LLC.

For more information about this book contact Lisa Akoury-Ross by email at
lross@SDPPublishing.com.

SDP Publishing
Permissions Department
PO Box 26, East Bridgewater, MA 02333
or email your request to info@SDPPublishing.com.

ISBN-13 (print): 978-0-9862896-4-4

ISBN (ebook): 978-0-9862896-5-1

Printed in the United States of America

Acknowledgments

A special thank you to the wonderful team at SDP Publishing and Eden Rivers Editorial for making this project a reality. Lisa A. and Lisa S., the dynamic duo, I would still be dreaming without your assistance; thank you for holding my hand every step of the way. Thank you to Randy Jennings for the most awesome illustrations a mother and son could ask for. And a special thank you to the expertise of Howard Johnson for helping to make this book come to life.

Thank you to Lenn for your constant inspiration, and to my mom for saying that if I didn't publish something I would be wasting my talents. Well, Mom, here is something.

Neta

To Lenn

Day is coming to an end.

Time to rest, time for bed.

"Brush your teeth, put on pajamas."
A good-night story to read with Mama.

"Race you to turn off the light!"

Hug and kiss and a wish good-night.

Mama leaves you all tucked in …

Crying, screaming, you begin:
"Sleep with me! I want you here.
You make the monsters disappear!"

10

11

"Should we look under the bed?"
Yes, you nod, your face all wet.

14

In the closet, behind the blinds,
not one monster in our sights.

Mama shakes her head and says,
"Big boys sleep in their beds.
Not with moms and not with dads."

19

One more hug and one more kiss.
"Back to bed, sir, if you please...!"

Dream of toys, and trains and trucks,
puppies, music, pancake stacks.

Happy dreams and dreams of joy,
nightly playmates for my boy.

Through the windows moonlight streams.
Eyes are closed … sleep, sweet dreams.

About The Author

Neta is a mom and a physician. She works and writes in sunny Arizona.

Big Boys Sleep in Their Beds

NETA FAYNBOYM

Also available in ebook format

TO PURCHASE:

Amazon.com

BarnesAndNoble.com

SDPPublishing.com

SDP Publishing

www.SDPPublishing.com

Contact us at: info@SDPPublishing.com

CPSIA information can be obtained
at www.ICGtesting.com
Printed in the USA
LVHW070959230519
618870LV00021B/170/P